THE PERFECT CHRISTMAS GIFT

by Judy Delton
illustrated by Lisa McCue

Macmillan Publishing Company   New York

Maxwell Macmillan Canada   Toronto

Maxwell Macmillan International

New York   Oxford   Singapore   Sydney

Text copyright © 1992 by Judy Delton
Illustrations copyright © 1992 by Lisa McCue

Macmillan Publishing Company is part of the Maxwell Communication Group of Companies.

Macmillan Publishing Company, 866 Third Avenue, New York, NY 10022.

Maxwell Macmillan Canada, Inc., 1200 Eglinton Avenue East, Suite 200, Don Mills, Ontario M3C 3N1.

First edition
Printed in Hong Kong by South China Printing Company (1988) Ltd.

1   3   5   7   9   10   8   6   4   2

The text of this book is set in 14 pt. ITC Zapf International Medium.
The illustrations are rendered in watercolor, acrylic, and colored pencil on bristol.

Library of Congress Cataloging-in-Publication Data
Delton, Judy. The perfect Christmas gift / by Judy Delton ; illustrated by Lisa McCue. — 1st ed.
p.   cm.   Summary: Bear is distressed by his inability to find the perfect Christmas present for Duck, until Rabbit points out that the true significance of the holiday is having friends.
ISBN 0-02-728471-9
[1. Gifts—Fiction.   2. Christmas—Fiction.   3. Friendship—Fiction.   4. Animals—Fiction.]   I. McCue, Lisa, ill.   II. Title.
PZ7.D388Pcl   1992   [E]—dc20   91-6549

Bear was on his way home from Mossy Mall. He was
carrying a large package. The snow was gently falling in
the woods and it was almost Christmas. When he came
to Rabbit's house, he decided to stop in for a rest.

"Rabbit!" he said, pounding on the door with his
elbow. There was a wreath on Rabbit's front door made
of carrot greens. "Wait till you see what I got Duck
for Christmas!"

Rabbit opened the door and invited Bear inside. The
snow blew in with a large gust of wind. Bear set his
package down on the floor and rubbed his paws
together. "I got Duck something she will really like!"
said Bear.

Rabbit walked around the large package, poking at the wrapping. Bear untied the string and opened it up.

"Just what Duck needs!" said Bear, pointing.

"A footstool!" said Rabbit.

"Not just any footstool, Rabbit," said Bear proudly. "This one is adjustable. It can go high or low."

Bear showed Rabbit how it worked. The two friends stood and admired it.

"Now when Duck is tired from working in her garden and picking all those apples from her tree," said Bear, "she can lean back and put her feet up. It will be very restful."

"It is just the right gift for Duck," agreed Rabbit.

Rabbit made a cup of tea and the friends sat at the
window looking out at the falling snow. As they
watched, they saw Duck come along the path. She was
carrying a large package.

Duck turned in at Rabbit's gate and knocked on
the door.

"Hello, Rabbit and Bear," she said when Rabbit
opened the door. She stamped the snow from her feet.
"I have just come from the sale at Mossy Mall. I bought
something I have wanted a long time."

Duck unwrapped the package she was carrying.
"A footstool!" she said proudly.

Bear's face fell. He pushed his own package in back
of his chair.

"Dear me," said Rabbit, frowning.

"This is not just *any* footstool," Duck went on. "It goes up and down. You can fix it just the way you want it." Duck showed them. Rabbit and Bear nodded. "What a lucky day for me!" said Duck, rewrapping her package and getting ready to leave.

Duck said good-bye and went out into the snowy woods. Rabbit shut the door. Bear looked as though he might cry.

"It was just what Duck wanted, you were right," said Rabbit sadly. "That is too bad, Bear."

"Well," said Bear, rewrapping the gift, "I will take it back to the store and try to find another gift for Duck."

The next morning Bear took the footstool back to the store. In the sporting goods department he saw a red bike on display. "This is just the right present for Duck," said Bear. "She will never buy one of these for herself."

Bear bought the bike and happily wheeled it home. Just as he was trying to wrap it, Rabbit came by.

"A bicycle!" said Rabbit. "That is a wonderful gift for Duck!"

"She can ride to the store on it," said Bear. "It has a basket for her to put things in."

Rabbit ran his paw over the shiny paint. "I can't wait to see her face on Christmas, Bear."

"That is what Christmas is for, Rabbit," said Bear warmly. "A time to surprise friends and make them happy."

"I think it is too big to wrap," frowned Rabbit, noticing that the paper kept sliding off the bike as Bear tried to cover it. "Maybe you can just put a ribbon on the handlebars."

"That is a good idea," said Bear. "I will just wheel it into the closet until Christmas."

Rabbit and Bear put the bike in the closet. It just fit. They could hardly close the door.

Just as Bear was buttering a muffin for Rabbit to have
with his tea, there was a knock on the front door.

"Bear," called Duck. "I wonder if I could borrow your
ladder. I am going to decorate my Christmas tree and I
can't reach the top to put the star on."

"Help yourself, Duck," called Bear, whose paws were
full of butter. "It's in the closet."

Duck opened the closet door to get out the ladder, and
then it was too late. Duck had seen the bike.

"I didn't know you had a bike," Duck said as she wheeled it out of the closet so that she could get out the ladder.

Bear ground his teeth together. He clenched his fists.

"That's a nice bike, Bear," said Duck, running her wing over the fender.

"Take the ladder, Duck," said Bear, handing it to her.

When Duck left, Bear kicked the back tire. Then he wheeled the bike to the front door.

"What a shame she saw it," said Rabbit. "But of course she doesn't know it is for *her*, Bear."

Bear shook his head. "Duck saw it," he said. "The bike is not a surprise now. Christmas has to be a surprise. I'm taking it back to the store, Rabbit."

Rabbit began to say that Duck could use a bike, but Bear would not listen. "It has to go back," he said.

Poor Bear, thought Rabbit, as he watched him trudge down the path to the mall. "He is having a terrible time with his Christmas shopping this year."

Rabbit finished his muffin and started for home.

On Christmas Eve the snow began to fall again.
Bear and Rabbit walked along the path to Duck's house.
They each carried presents tied with red ribbons.

"Duck will never guess what I got her," said Bear.
"I know she doesn't have one. It will be useful, and it
will be a big, big surprise."

When they got to Duck's house there was a fire in the fireplace. The tree was decorated with bright lights and silver tinsel and colorful ornaments. Good smells were coming from Duck's kitchen.

The three friends had a good dinner. Bear leaned back in his chair and sighed. He patted his stomach. "You are a good cook, Duck. That was the best apple pie I have ever eaten."

The friends sang carols around the tree. Then they fed the hungry birds in Duck's backyard. And then Rabbit said, "I think it is time to open our gifts!"

"I can't wait," said Bear.

The friends tore open the boxes with their names on them. There were warm winter caps for Bear and Duck from Rabbit.

"I knit them myself," said Rabbit proudly. "I knew you needed them."

Soon all of the gifts were opened but one. "This is for you, Duck," said Bear. "You will never guess what it is in a million years."

Bear and Rabbit waited while Duck tore off the paper. She unwrapped something long and thin. On one end was a wire basket.

"What is it?" asked Duck.

"It is an apple picker," said Bear. "You can reach the apples on the top of your tree, Duck. You will not need a ladder. You don't have an apple picker already, do you?"

"No, I don't, Bear."

"Are you surprised?" asked Rabbit.

"Why, yes, I'm very surprised," said Duck.

"Good," said Rabbit with relief.

"Next fall you will have your apples picked in no time," said Bear.

Duck shook her head. "No I won't," she said sadly. "I don't have an apple tree anymore, Bear. It blew down in the wind storm last week."

Bear put his head in his paws. He looked like he was about to cry.

"But it is a wonderful apple picker!" said Duck. "And I will plant another apple tree in spring."

"It is a bad gift," sobbed Bear. "An apple picker is not a good gift if you don't have apples."

Duck gave Bear a hug. "It is the thought that counts," she said.

"You *could* use it for your clothespins, Duck," said Rabbit. "Or to carry your letters to the post office."

Bear sobbed harder.

"Bear," said Rabbit, "Gifts are not the most important thing about Christmas. Neither are surprises. The most important thing is having friends. We are with friends, Bear! This is no time to feel sorry for yourself. I think we should go sliding on the hill in Duck's backyard."

Bear took out his handkerchief and blew his nose. "You are right," he said. "The best Christmas gift is you and Duck."

The three friends put on heavy clothes. Bear and Duck wore the new caps that Rabbit had knit them. Then they all went out into the snowy night and coasted down Duck's icy hill. After that they built a snowman. When it got dark they went back into Duck's house and drank hot cocoa in front of the fire. They looked at the lights twinkling on the tree.

"I have it!" said Duck, snapping her wing feathers.
"Tomatoes! I can pick tomatoes without going outdoors.
I can pick them right through my window with your
gift, Bear!"

"If it rains, you won't get wet!" shouted Rabbit.

"Your feet won't get dirty on that muddy path,"
said Bear.

"What a fine Christmas," said Duck, her feet up on her
adjustable footstool.

"The best Christmas ever," said Bear.